```
J796.357
RAM     Rambeck, Richard
          History of the Minnesota Twins
```

Spirit Lake Accelerated Reader

Level 8.7   Points 1.0
       6.6

			not	H-LP
			"	0

WITHDRAWN

SPIRIT LAKE PUBLIC LIBRARY
SPIRIT LAKE IOWA 51360

DEMCO

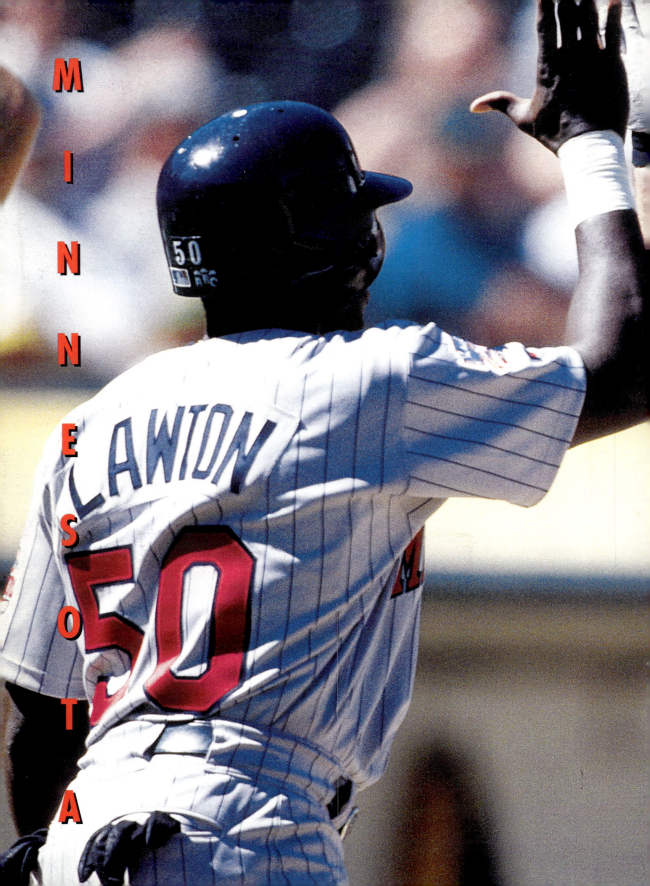

RICHARD RAMBECK

THE HISTORY OF THE
TWINS

CREATIVE EDUCATION

Published by Creative Education
123 South Broad Street, Mankato, Minnesota 56001
Creative Education is an imprint of The Creative Company

Designed by Rita Marshall
Editorial assistance by Michael Welch & John Nichols

Photos by: Allsport Photography, AP/Wide World, Corbis-Bettmann,
Fotosport, SportsChrome.

Copyright © 1999 Creative Education.
International copyrights reserved in all countries.
No part of this book may be reproduced in any form without written
permission from the publisher.
Printed in the United States of America.

Library of Congress Cataloging-in-Publication Data

Rambeck, Richard.
The History of the Minnesota Twins / by Richard Rambeck.
p. cm. — (Baseball)
Summary: A team history of the Minnesota Twins, a franchise begun as the
Washington Senators, but resident of the Twin Cities area since 1961.
ISBN: 0-88682-914-3

1. Minnesota Twins (Baseball team)—History—Juvenile literature.
[1. Minnesota Twins (Baseball team)—History. 2. Baseball—History.]
I. Title. II. Series: Baseball (Mankato, Minn.)

GV875.M55R36   1999
796.357'64'09776579—dc21   97-9232

9 8 7 6 5 4 3 2

Minnesota's Twin Cities—Minneapolis and St. Paul—are the two largest towns in the land known both as the North Star State and the Gopher State. The Twin Cities metropolitan area accounts for more than half of the 4.3 million people who live in Minnesota. The state is known for its strong agricultural roots and its equally progressive footing in modern industry. Perhaps Minnesota's finest quality, however, is that it offers citizens and visitors alike the richest variety of outdoor experiences—from warm summers filled with camping and boating on the countless rivers and lakes,

Hall-of-Famer Harmon Killebrew.

Camilo Pascual led the Minnesota pitching staff in victories, earned run average, and strikeouts.

to cold, snowy winters when skiing, figure-skating, and hockey become the activities of choice.

The Twin Cities area is also home to a rich sports tradition that includes the Minnesota Vikings of the National Football League; the Minnesota Timberwolves of the National Basketball Association; the Minnesota Wild of the National Hockey League, which begins play in the year 2000; and major league baseball's Minnesota Twins, a team that has been an American League fixture since 1961. The Minnesota baseball franchise actually began in Washington, D.C., as the Senators, but team owner Calvin Griffith felt that fans in the nation's capital weren't supportive enough. He moved the team to Minnesota, where they became the Twins.

From the very beginning, the Twins and the people of Minnesota built a passionate relationship. More than 24,000 showed up for a chilly Opening Day in 1961, and the Twins drew nearly 1.5 million fans their first year playing in Metropolitan Stadium.

Since that initial opening day, there have been good times and bad for the Twins. Stars like Rod Carew and Kirby Puckett have come and gone, and the torch has now been passed to a new group of heroes. Players like 1995 Rookie of the Year Marty Cordova and 20-game winner Brad Radke will write the future chapters of Twins success. But to many fans, the team's first star still shines brightest in their memories. Harmon Killebrew built professional baseball in Minnesota one mammoth home run at a time.

Up-and-coming second baseman Todd Walker.

"The Killer" hammers homers

1 9 6 4

Harmon Killebrew set a Minnesota record by belting 49 home runs during the season.

Although Minnesota wasn't a championship-caliber ballclub at first, the team did bring several budding stars with it from Washington. The best of these was a stocky, muscular slugger named Harmon Killebrew. Killebrew began his major-league career in 1954, when he was just 17 years old. He soon established himself as one of the finest home-run hitters in baseball. Killebrew led the American League in homers five times during his years with the Twins, including three straight seasons from 1962 through 1964.

The gentlemanly Killebrew was ironically nicknamed "the Killer." His deadly effect on baseballs struck fear in the hearts of pitchers everywhere. The former Idaho farmboy had a no-nonsense approach to hitting. While waiting in the on-deck circle, he would stand virtually motionless and glare at the pitcher. Then he would take three or four ferocious swings before kneeling and resuming his glare. Once in the batter's box, the right-handed hitter would allow himself one calming swish of the bat between pitches. Otherwise, he stood absolutely still, with the bat resting on his shoulder.

"I'm not a fidgety person," Killebrew explained. "I try to stay as calm and relaxed as I can. It helps me concentrate, which I think is the most important thing about hitting."

Killebrew's trademark remained the long ball throughout his brilliant career. He wound up hitting 573 home runs, making him fifth on the list of all-time home run hitters. He slammed a homer an average of once every 12.9 times at bat—just a notch behind Babe Ruth's record of one every

11.8 times up. In 1984, Killebrew was named to the Baseball Hall of Fame.

Killebrew wasn't the Twins' only outstanding hitter in the 1960s, however. Right fielder Tony Oliva made a tremendous debut by winning the American League batting title in 1964. (He repeated the feat in 1965.) For his debut efforts, Oliva was named the American League Rookie of the Year. Both Killebrew and Oliva had outstanding years in 1965, but shortstop Zoilo Versalles had the season of a lifetime. The speedster led the American League in runs scored (126) and doubles (45). He finished second in triples (12) and third in stolen bases (27). To no one's surprise, Versalles was named the American League Most Valuable Player.

The Twins posted a 102–60 record in 1965, which is still a franchise record for victories in a season, and won the American League pennant. It was the first time in six years that a team other than the New York Yankees had won the American League title. The Twins had aced out one team with a rich tradition for the pennant and faced another proud team in the World Series—the Los Angeles Dodgers. If the Twins were in awe of the powerful Dodgers, it didn't show. Minnesota won the first two games of the series at home, defeating Los Angeles pitching aces Don Drysdale and Sandy Koufax in the process. Los Angeles then won all three games at home and returned to Minnesota with a 3–2 lead in the series. The Twins rebounded for a 5–1 victory in game six, but Koufax tossed a shutout in the seventh game as the Dodgers took the series with a 2–0 victory.

Twins shortstop Zoilo Versalles was named the AL MVP for leading Minnesota to their first pennant.

1987 World Series hero Frank Viola.

Another hard-throwing pitcher, Scott Erickson.

CAREW HITS AND HITS AND HITS

1 9 6 9

In his first and last year as manager, Billy Martin led the Twins to the AL West title.

The young Twins had been beaten, but they were determined to get back to the World Series. It seemed as if they would have plenty of chances, with such hitting stars as Killebrew, Versalles, and Oliva and fielders like Earl Battey and Bob Allison. The pitching staff was ably manned by Jim "Mudcat" Grant, Jim Perry, Dean Chance, and Jim Kaat. As if that weren't enough talent, the Twins found another star in 1967, a sweet-swinging second baseman named Rod Carew.

Carew showed his awesome potential immediately as he was named the American League Rookie of the Year in 1967. His intelligent hitting approach and superb bat control baffled opposing pitchers, and in 1969, the left-handed hitter from Panama won the first of seven batting titles as a Minnesota player. "Rod Carew could get more hits with a soup bone than I could get with a rack full of bats," joked teammate Steve Brye. "He can do anything he wants to up there."

Carew often said his favorite kind of hit was one "just one inch or two outside a guy's reach. Maybe he cheated over a step in the other direction on me, and I kept him honest. I hit the ball to the opposite field so much that sometimes they'll move everybody to the left side against me. But I just take my natural swing."

Like Carew, Harmon Killebrew had an outstanding 1969 season. The 32-year-old slugger topped the league in homers with 49, and he led the league in runs batted in with 140. He was named the American League Most Valuable Player, and his heroics sparked the Twins to the AL West Division title. (The league was split into two divisions in 1969

12

after the addition of two expansion franchises.) Minnesota advanced to play in the American League Championship Series against East Division winner Baltimore. The powerful Orioles had registered 109 victories during the regular season, 12 more than the Twins. Minnesota wasn't expected to give the Orioles much trouble, and the Twins didn't, losing the best-of-five series in three straight.

Minnesota came back stronger in 1970, taking the AL West with a 98–64 record, but the team once again ran head-first into the Baltimore Orioles in the league championship series. Baltimore dispatched the Twins and went on to claim the World Series title. "We had some great ballclubs back then," said a proud Killebrew. "But Baltimore always had our number."

Rod Carew led the Twins in hitting for the first of seven straight seasons.

Minnesota's string of success would come to an end, and the franchise would have to wait 17 years for its next taste of the postseason. Twins stars such as Killebrew and Jim Perry grew old, and in Oliva's case, a series of crippling knee injuries shortened a brilliant career. Minnesota soon fell behind rising powers Oakland and Kansas City in the AL West. The Twins staggered to a 74–86 record in 1971, despite a remarkable year from Oliva. The hobbled slugger hit .337—a career high—and won his third and final American League batting title.

The following year, Rod Carew succeeded Oliva as AL batting champ, a title Carew would hold five more times in the next six years. Carew and Dutch-born pitcher Bert Blyleven provided many of the highlights for the Twins, whose glory years slipped further and further behind them.

In the late 1970s, Minnesota owner Calvin Griffith began

In his first full season with the Twins, Kent Hrbek was named to the AL All-Star team.

to sell most of his high-paid veterans and replace them with younger players who had low salaries. Griffith also made no effort to try to acquire quality players as free agents. As a result, attendance at Metropolitan Stadium dropped as fast as the team's fortunes.

As the 1980s approached, the Twins were going nowhere. Carew, who was voted American League MVP in 1977 after hitting an amazing .388, was traded to the California Angels in 1979. The Twins celebrated their 20th season in 1981, but the team wound up in last place.

Then, just as it started to look as if Minnesota would never recover, the team's luck began to change. With the addition of a lanky first baseman from the nearby suburb of Bloomington, Minnesota, and a fireplug outfielder from the projects of Chicago, the first seeds of a championship were planted.

"HERBIE" AND KIRBY SPARK TWINS REVIVAL

Kent Hrbek was born in Minneapolis on May 21, 1960. Twenty-one years later, he was on the verge of joining his hometown major-league team. The slugging first baseman was playing for Visalia of the California League in 1981 when the power-starved Twins called him up. "The last week before I was called up [to the majors], this clothing store [in Visalia] had a promotion in which it would give away a pair of pants to the first player who hit a home run in a game," Hrbek laughed. "I think I won four pairs that week. I had to order them by phone, though, because I was already in the major leagues."

Hrbek's first action came against the New York Yankees in

Ten-time All-Star Kirby Puckett.

Kirby Puckett, who would be named to 10 All-Star teams, played his first season with the Twins.

historic Yankee Stadium. With the score tied in the 12th inning the starstruck rookie strode to the plate. "I remember being real nervous when I was in the on-deck circle but I didn't want anybody to know it," laughed Hrbek. "So I tried to act cool, but inside I was a basket case." Hrbek managed to shake off his nerves long enough to blast a home run that eventually won the game for the Twins. "What a way to start a career," said Hrbek. "I don't think my feet touched the ground all the way around the bases."

Minnesota teammates called Hrbek "the Kid," but this kid was hitting like a man. His performance at the end of the 1981 season earned him a spot on the Twins' roster for 1982, which was also the year the Twins moved into a new home: the Hubert H. Humphrey Metrodome, a sturdy, weatherproof structure that featured a 10-acre roof made of Teflon-coated fiberglass. The team's home park was new, but the results were the same. The rookie-laden club finished the season with a 60–102 record, worst in the major leagues.

Hrbek was one of the few Twins capable of terrorizing opposing pitchers. His .301 average, 23 homers, and 92 RBIs were a bright spot in an otherwise down year for the team, but help was soon on the way. In the 1982 amateur draft, the Twins selected a stocky little outfielder by the name of Kirby Puckett. It would prove to be one of the best choices the team ever made.

The 5-foot-9 and 220-pound Puckett seemed an unlikely ballplayer, but from the moment he made it to the majors in 1984, he punished American League pitching. In Puckett's first game, the Chicago native smoked four hits in five at-bats against the California Angels and never slowed down from there. Puckett went on to collect 2,304 hits, 207 homers, and 1,085 RBIs, while hitting .318 during his 12-year career. "Scouts would always tell me I was too short, or too heavy, or too whatever," joked the stocky outfielder. "But baseball isn't about being a size or a shape. It's about how big you are inside that counts."

Indeed, Twins fans fell instantly for the big-hearted, fun-loving Puckett. Whether he was scorching line drives or leaping high up the center-field wall to make dramatic, game-saving catches, he was always the same old "Puck." "I think the fans like me because they can tell I love the game and I have fun when I play," observed Puckett. "I'm just a regular guy who just happens to play baseball."

With Hrbek and Puckett to anchor the team, and other rising stars like third baseman Gary Gaetti, right fielder Tom Brunansky, and pitcher Frank Viola contributing, the Twins began to improve. The offense was always formidable. In 1986, Hrbek, Puckett, Gaetti, and Brunansky alone combined for 107 homers and 380 RBIs, but the team's pitching staff was one of the league's worst. When the Twins sank back to last place in '86, it became evident that some changes needed to be made. One of the biggest would be the naming of Minnesota native Tom Kelly as manager.

Right fielder Tom Brunansky led the Twins for the season by slamming 27 home runs.

T.K.'S BOYS TAKE IT ONE GAME AT A TIME

There was a different attitude in the Twins' training camp in 1987. In large part, it was due to new manager Tom Kelly, who, at the age of 36, was the youngest skipper in the majors. "I like to keep the game fun," the low-key Kelly

1991 Rookie of the Year Chuck Knoblauch (pages 18-19).

1986

Gary Gaetti led the club with 34 homers and 108 RBIs, and he picked up his first Gold Glove award.

explained. One of the reasons Kelly expected the game to be fun for the Twins was the acquisition of ace relief pitcher Jeff Reardon from the Montreal Expos. "Remember," Kelly recalled before the season started, "this club lost 27 games last year from the seventh inning on. If Reardon can close the door for us this year, we think the rest of our lineup can have a lot more fun, too."

Kelly proved to be a prophet. Reardon—known as "the Terminator" for his ability to close games—notched 31 saves, and he complemented an improved staff of starting pitchers led by lefty Frank Viola (17–10, 2.90 earned-run average) and right-hander Bert Blyleven (15–12). The Twins also got great years from Puckett (.332 average, 28 homers, 99 RBIs), Hrbek (.285 average, 34 homers, 90 RBIs), Gaetti (31 homers, 109 RBIs), and Brunansky (32 homers, 85 RBIs). "We just do what T.K. [Kelly] tells us," observed Puckett. "Don't get too high or too low, just go out, give 100 percent and we'll win the battle one game at a time." Minnesota wound up capturing its first AL West Division title in 17 years, posting an 85–77 record.

In the American League Championship Series, the Twins weren't expected to do well against the Detroit Tigers, who had won 98 games. But Minnesota captured the first two games in the Metrodome, and the Tigers never recovered. After beating Detroit four games to one, the Twins advanced to their first World Series in 22 years. Again, no one expected Minnesota to beat the powerful St. Louis Cardinals. But the Twins had two things going for them: the Metrodome and the thousands of screaming fans packed inside waving Homer Hankies at each game.

During the 1987 World Series, history was made. For the first time, World Series games were played indoors. And the Metrodome wasn't just any dome; it was such a noisy place, the Cardinals absolutely hated to play there—especially after losing 10–1 and 8–4 in the first two games. Luckily for the Cards, the series then shifted to Busch Stadium in St. Louis, where the home team won games three, four, and five to take a 3–2 lead. Back in the Metrodome, the Cardinals streaked to a 5–2 lead in game six and were on the verge of closing out the series. Then, Twins designated hitter Don Baylor stepped up and slammed a two-run homer in the fifth inning to spark a comeback. An inning later, Kent Hrbek supplied the biggest blow of the series, a grand-slam home run that gave the Twins a commanding 10–5 lead. Minnesota wound up winning 11–5.

At age 37, Tom Kelly became the youngest manager to lead a team to the AL Championship Series.

Manager Tom Kelly then gave Viola—winner in game one, loser in game four—the starting call in game seven. The Twins' ace gave up two runs in the second inning, but that was all he would surrender. Minnesota scored single runs in the second, fifth, sixth, and eighth innings to claim a 4–2 victory and the first World Series title in Minnesota history. Viola was named series MVP, and the Metrodome, where the Twins won all four games, was clearly baseball's MVS—Most Valuable Stadium.

The next year, Minnesota's record improved to 91–71, and the Twins became the first AL club to draw more than three million fans in a season. But the team finished a distant second to a powerful Oakland squad.

In 1989 and '90 Puckett and Hrbek continued to produce big numbers, but the Twins began to slide back in the stand-

Jeff Reardon, "The Terminator."

ings. The pitching staff had fallen from World Series heights to being 11th in the league in 1990. The drop was due largely to the trades of Blyleven and Viola for younger, unproven pitchers who had to learn on the job. "We just aren't getting it done on the mound," explained Kelly. "But hopefully the lumps we take now will pay off down the road." The Twins' poor pitching doomed them to a last place 74–88 record in 1990.

The next season didn't start much better. The Twins were in sixth place by late May. But a 15-game winning streak in June started Minnesota toward a 95–67 regular-season record and a meeting with the Toronto Blue Jays in the American League Championship Series.

Led by Puckett, Hrbek, and veteran pitcher Jack Morris, a St. Paul native who had been signed before the 1991 season, the Twins manhandled the Jays. After the two teams split a pair at the Metrodome, Minnesota swept three games at the Skydome, then prepared to face the Atlanta Braves in the World Series.

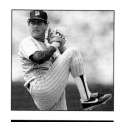

Frank Viola was honored with the Cy Young Award as the AL's outstanding pitcher, going 24–7 with a 2.64 ERA.

THE GREATEST WORLD SERIES EVER

Like the Twins, the Braves had gone from last in their division in 1990 to first in 1991. Atlanta was stocked with talent, but Minnesota's team was even better than the one that had scrapped its way to a championship four years earlier. In addition to Puckett, Hrbek, and Morris, the Twins had a 20-game winner in young pitcher Scott Erickson and a proven closer in Rick Aguilera. Kevin Tapani gave Minnesota another solid starting pitcher, Chili Davis led the team with

After winning 17 games, Allan Anderson became the AL's winningest pitcher over the '88 and '89 seasons.

93 RBIs in the regular season, and second baseman Chuck Knoblauch had earned the AL Rookie of the Year award with his fiery play.

The Braves and the Twins kept the fans on the edge of their seats throughout a series that featured five one-run victories, four games won on the final at-bat, and three contests that went into extra innings.

Just as they had in 1987, the Twins took the first two games at the Metrodome. Afterward, Atlanta catcher and Minnesota native Greg Olson said, "It's nice to be in Minnesota. But I'm ready to leave." The Braves won the next three games at home and returned to the dreaded Metrodome needing only one more victory to take the World Series crown.

Clutch hitter Randy Bush.

Before game six, Kirby Puckett told his teammates that he'd carry them to victory. "We were all real tight, then Puck comes into the clubhouse and tells us all not to worry; he said, 'Just get on the bus. I'm driving,'" laughed teammate Gene Larkin. "Did he ever." In the third inning, Puckett's perfectly timed leap against the left center-field wall took away a sure extra-base hit from Ron Gant. Then, with the score tied in the 11th inning, Puckett crushed a home run that won the game, tied the series, and cemented his standing as the most beloved figure in Minnesota sports. As Puckett's homer cleared the wall, TV announcer Jack Buck exclaimed, "We'll see you tomorrow night!"

St. Paul native Jack Morris returned home to win 18 games for the Minnesota club.

"It's a storybook World Series," said an ecstatic Tom Kelly in the Minnesota locker room after the game. "What's going to happen tomorrow in game seven, chapter seven? Oh my, I can't wait."

The final game lived up to the Twins' manager's expectations. As the game progressed, Minnesota's Jack Morris and Atlanta's John Smoltz each proved unhittable. The score remained tied at 0–0 as both teams squandered chances to bring runners home. Kelly told Morris after the ninth that Aguilera would be called on to pitch the 10th, but the fiery Morris insisted on returning to the mound. "I would have needed a shotgun to get him out of the game," said Kelly. "And I didn't have one."

The Twins won in the bottom of the 10th when Larkin, pinch-hitting, singled to score Dan Gladden, who jumped on home plate with both feet while his teammates—led by an ecstatic Morris—mobbed him.

Fay Vincent, commissioner of baseball at the time, said it

1995 Rookie of the Year Marty Cordova (pages 26-27).

best when he proclaimed, "It was probably the greatest World Series ever."

CHANGES SIGNAL THE END OF AN ERA

Intense closer Rick Aguilera saved 41 games with a 2.84 ERA as the Twins posted a solid 90–72 record.

Just months after the thrill of the Twins' second World Series championship, Twins fans were deflated when Jack Morris signed with Toronto for more money. And though Minnesota had a strong 1992 season, the Twins have since suffered through losing seasons, finishing last or next-to-last each year in the new AL Central Division. (Both major leagues were divided into three divisions in 1994.)

But fans could always count on catching the Kirby and "Herbie" show down at the Dome—at least they could until August 4, 1994. That day, Kent Hrbek announced that he would retire at the end of the season—which came sooner than anyone expected because the players went on strike just one week later. In 1990, Hrbek had turned down the chance to make more money playing somewhere else in order to stay with Minnesota. "I was born a Twin, and I'll die a Twin," he said.

But while Hrbek was able to choose his time of departure, his longtime friend and teammate, Kirby Puckett, had to leave the game two years later because of circumstances beyond his control.

On the morning of March 28, 1996, Puckett woke up and discovered that he couldn't see well out of his right eye. For months, fans prayed that the condition would improve and Puckett (who also had turned down more money to play elsewhere) would be able to return to the game he loved so much. But on July 12, "Puck" announced that the condition, an eye disease called glaucoma, would prevent him from ever seeing well enough to play baseball again.

In September, more than 51,000 people packed the Metrodome to thank Puckett for 12 years of amazing baseball and to reassure him that his devotion, warmth, and generosity had earned him a permanent place in the heart of the community. "All I wanted to do was just play baseball," Puckett said after the event. "I never thought about anything like this."

Puckett's appeal had as much to do with his ball-playing ability as it did with his attitude toward the game. In reflecting on Puckett's playing career, Jim Souhan of the *Star Tribune* newspaper wrote: "What Puckett meant to the Twins transcended statistics."

Marty Cordova homered in five consecutive games, tying a club record and setting a major-league record for rookies.

FACING AN UNCERTAIN FUTURE

By the mid- and late 1990s, the Twins had fallen into the unenviable situation that frustrates many small-market teams: always coming up one or two players short of playoff contention. The team's overall performance has left it out of postseason play since 1991.

Not that there haven't been highlights worth cheering in recent years: Scott Erickson's no-hitter against Milwaukee in April 1994, outfielder Marty Cordova's AL Rookie of the Year season in 1995, and Dave Winfield's and Paul Molitor's milestones of 3,000 hits while wearing Twins uniforms in 1993 and 1996 respectively.

Twins fans definitely have enjoyed watching the on-the-field performances of great Minnesota-native players like

Twenty-game winner Brad Radke.

Paul Molitor: 3,000 hits and counting.

Fans expected LaTroy Hawkins' strength and stability to lead him to a dynamic season with the Twins.

Winfield, Molitor, and catcher Terry Steinbach, each of whom has chosen to come home and don the Twins' uniform in the later stages of their careers.

However, it's unclear whether natives will always have that opportunity. Twins owner Carl Pohlad has said that a new stadium is necessary in order to keep the team in Minnesota. Several proposals have been discussed, but the issue is still undecided.

Wherever the Twins are playing, the team will have more rebuilding years ahead of it. Knoblauch was traded in the off-season for two pitchers, Eric Milton and Danny Mota, along with minor-leaguers Brian Buchanan and shortstop Christian Guzman. Veterans like Molitor and Steinbach set a sterling example for the Twins' many inexperienced but talented players like infielder Todd Walker and pitchers Brad Radke and LaTroy Hawkins.

The team's weakness is once again a lack of pitching depth. Radke won 20 games in 1997 and closer Rick Aguilera piled up 26 saves, but Hawkins and veteran Bob Tewksbury will have to improve in order for the Twins to be contenders again. "A lot of experts wrote us off when we finished last in 1986 and 1990 too," noted Kelly. "We've got impact guys, but things just have to break right, and our young guys have to come through."

For Kelly and the Twins, the task of becoming a contender again is sure to be difficult, but not impossible or unprecedented. "We've done it before, and with a little luck, we'll do it again," said the Twins manager. "We just have to be patient." Fans in Minnesota know that when it comes to World Series championships, the thrill is worth the wait.